TEN ROSY ROSES

For Russell—
My wild climbing rose
—J.G.

Text copyright © 1999 by Dee Michel & Guy Michel
Illustrations copyright © 1999 by Julia Gorton
Printed in the U.S.A. All rights reserved. http://www.harperchildrens.com
Library of Congress Cataloging-in-Publication Data   Merriam, Eve, date
Ten rosy roses / by Eve Merriam ; pictures by Julia Gorton   p.   cm.
Summary: Ten rosy roses stand in a line until, one by one, ten children
pick them.   ISBN 0-06-027887-0. — ISBN 0-06-027888-9 (lib. bdg.)
1. Counting-out rhymes.   2. Children's poetry, American.   [1. Counting.
2. Roses—Poetry.   3. American poetry.]   I. Gorton, Julia, ill.   II. Title.
PS3525.E639T46   1999   98-27473   811'.54[E]—dc21   CIP   AC
Designed by Julia Gorton
1   2   3   4   5   6   7   8   9   10
❖
First Edition

TEN ROSY ROSES

Eve Merriam
illustrations by Julia Gorton

HarperCollins*Publishers*

10

Ten rosy roses

standing in a line,

9

Jan picks one and now there are nine.

8

Nine rosy roses near the garden gate,

Nina picks one and now there are eight.

Eight rosy roses, along comes Kevin,
he picks one and now there are seven.

7

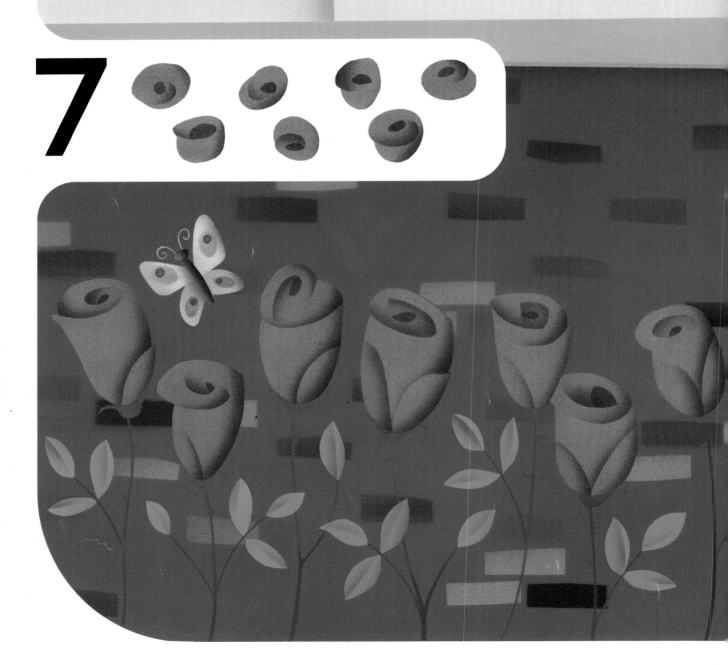

Seven rosy roses by the wall of bricks,

Pam picks one and now there are six.

5

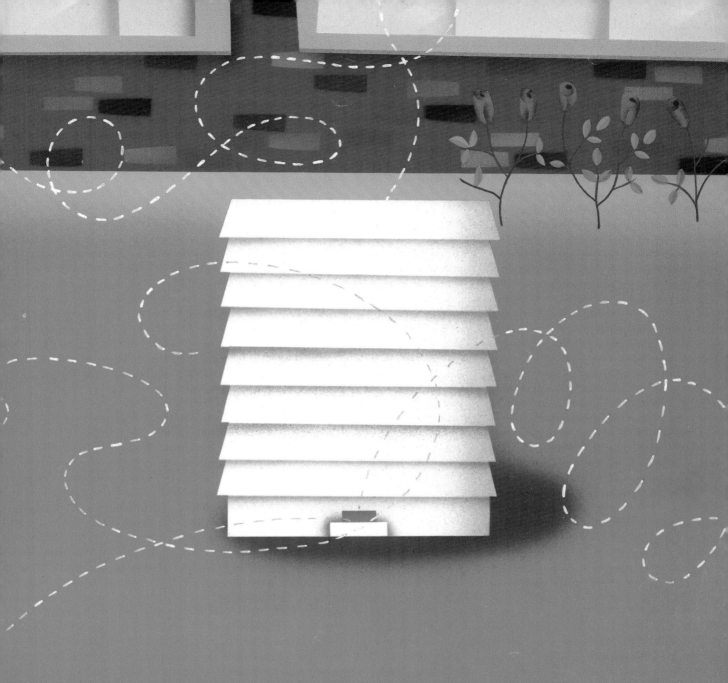

Six rosy roses beyond the honey hive,

Helen picks one and now there are five.

Five rosy roses at the schoolhouse door,

Kim picks one and now there are four.

Four rosy roses near the maple tree,
Amos picks one and now there are three.

Three rosy roses beneath a sky of blue,

Rachel picks one and now there are two.

Two rosy roses standing in the sun, the

0

twins take a turn and now there are none.

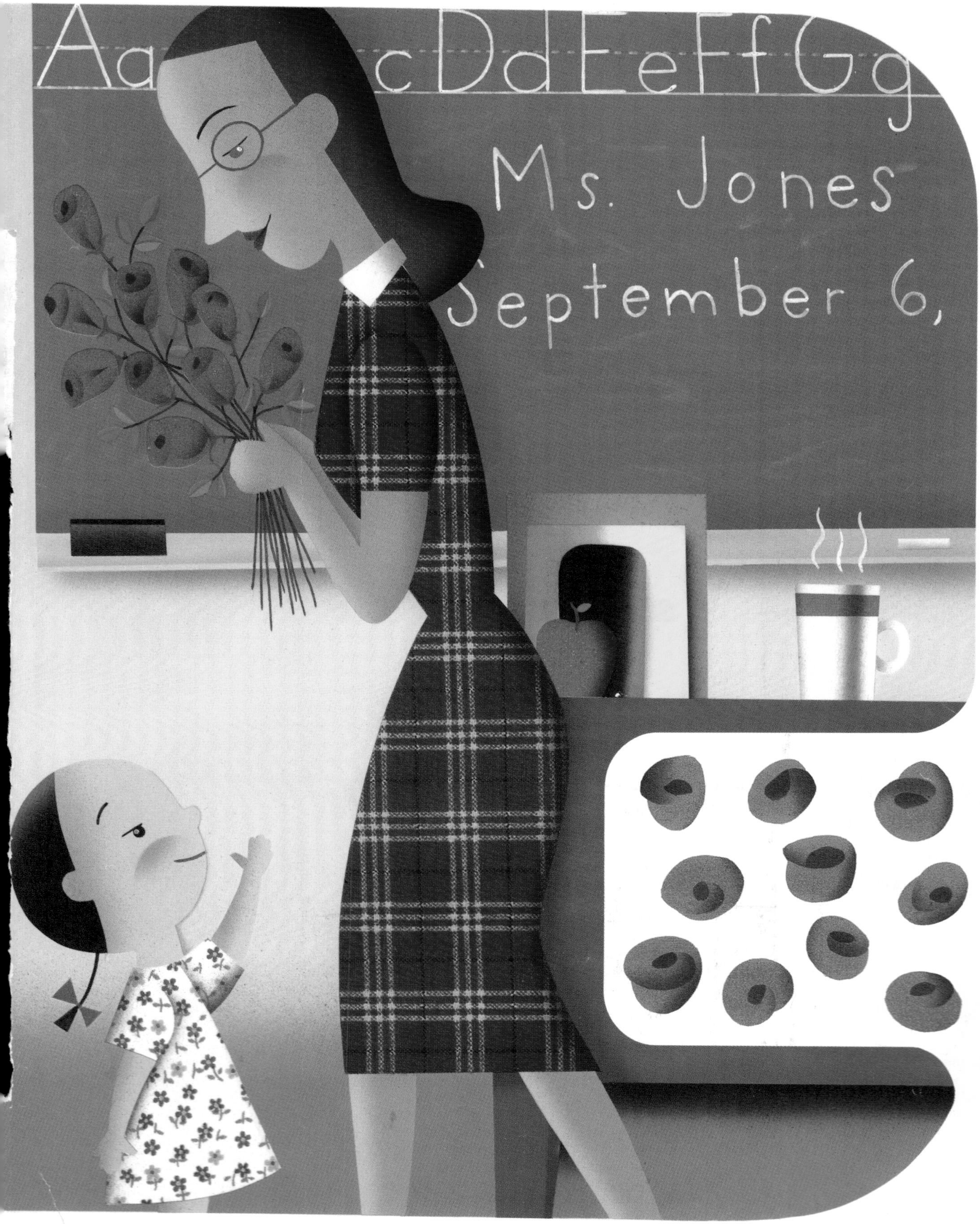

Aa cDdEeFfGg
Ms. Jones
September 6,